A Dog Called You

Alison Prince was born in Beckenham, Kent, of a Scottish mother and Yorkshire father. She won a scholarship to the Slade School of Fine Art and began a teaching career on leaving college, but soon moved into freelance writing and illustration. She has written over thirty books for young people, and *The Sherwood Hero* won the Guardian Children's Fiction Award. She lives in Scotland, on the Isle of Arran, and has three grown-up children.

ALISON PRINCE

A Dog Called You

MACMILLAN CHILDREN'S BOOKS

First published 1993 by Macmillan Children's Books

This edition produced 2001 for
The Book People Ltd,
Hall Wood Avenue,
Haydock,
St Helens WA11 9UL

ISBN 0 330 32708 9

A CIP catalogue record for this book is available from
the British Library.

Phototypeset by Intype, London
Printed and bound in Great Britain by
Mackays of Chatham plc, Chatham, Kent

Chapter 1

Barney had an old van which squeaked
and rattled. In it, he had a lot of old rope,
a machine for sharpening knives, a lawn-
mower and a hedge-trimmer, a spade and
some sacks and various bits of car
engines. He had a big frying pan with a
wooden handle, a black kettle, a tin-
opener and a sleeping-bag. And he had a
dog.

"Hey, you," Barney would say as he
finished his supper beside the van,
"Catch!" And he would throw the dog half
a sausage roll or a bit of left-over rabbit
or whatever he had. Sometimes there
would be some butcher's scraps or a
meaty bone.

The dog thought of himself as You. That was the sound of his name. "You, get in the van," Barney would say. Or, when You barked at a policeman, "Shut up, you." Otherwise, he didn't take much notice of him. Barney was a bit short-sighted, and one dog looked much like another to him.

You was an untidy sort of dog with brown fur and big feet. He liked Barney, and stayed with him for most of the time, sleeping beside him on an old sack in the van if it was raining, or beside him on the grass in the warm summer nights.

But there were times when You was bored.

He was bored in the oily-smelling scrapyards where Barney haggled with men in boiler suits about the prices of bits of cars.

He was bored in pubs, where Barney
played darts and tried to make people
agree that he could mow their lawns or
trim their hedges.

5

He was bored when he sat on the
pavement beside the knife-sharpening
machine, and he hated the noise it made
when Barney held a knife to its wheel
and the sparks flew.

6

At such times, You would get up and shuffle off to try and find something to eat. He thought of it as a kind of game, because people took great care of their food and tried their best not to let him have it. He got chased out of supermarkets, and women shouted at him for trying to rootle in their shopping trolleys.

Children would sometimes share an ice cream with him, but their mothers got cross with them for doing that. The best bet, You found, was to crouch among the ducks in the park while people threw bread to them. Sometimes, if he was in luck, they threw bits of pork pie as well.

Or he would sit in front of people eating
sandwiches on a bench, staring at them
and dribbling, until they gave him a bit.

Chapter 2

One hot day, after a happy time in a
dustbin at the back of a Greek
restaurant, You lay down on the
pavement and licked the last of the
taramasalata off his paws, then went to
sleep. He was woken by a voice just above
his head.

"Poor thing!" the voice said.

"*Poor* thing," agreed another one.

You opened one eye and saw two little
girls gazing down at him and looking
sad.

He shut his eye again. And then, to his surprise, the little girls bent down and got hold of him. They picked him up, with rather a struggle, and lugged him all the way home.

"Mummy!" they said. "This poor dog was lying on the pavement. We think he's ill." They stood You on the floor very carefully and he shook himself, then went and sniffed in the kitchen bin.

"Nothing wrong with *him*," said the little girls' mother. "And you shouldn't touch strange dogs. We'll take him back where you found him – his owner is probably hunting for him everywhere."

You lay down on the floor again and sighed. Conversation bored him. The little girls' mother looked at him doubtfully.

"Well," she said, "perhaps he *is* a bit hungry. He could have that left-over shepherd's pie."

You wolfed down the shepherd's pie and two chocolate biscuits, and then the little girls and their mother took him back to the pavement outside the Greek restaurant and left him there. "Goodbye, dog," they said.

You gave them a wag of his tail, then went home to Barney's van.

"Hello, you," said Barney, and gave him the last of his take-away tandoori chicken and chips.

Chapter 3

The next afternoon, as You sat and waited
for Barney to finish mowing somebody's
grass, he thought about the little girls and
the chocolate biscuits (not to mention the
tandoori chicken and chips), and had a
good idea. Leaving Barney mowing, he
trotted off to the shopping centre and lay
down on the pavement with his eyes
shut.

He lay there for quite some time, hoping
to be noticed, then at last he heard the
words, "Poor thing!"

You raised his head a little, then let it
flop back on the pavement pathetically.
The young man who had spoken to him
carried a basketful of vegetables. He
didn't smell of shepherd's pie or tandoori,
but You wasn't fussy.

14

The young man put his basket down,
then stooped and, with some difficulty,
gathered You into his arms. Then he
staggered home with dog and basket, and

put You gently down in the kitchen. You found a saucer of milk on the floor, and some left-over cat food, and tidied it all up while the cat leapt on the draining board and spat.

"Poor thing," the young man said again. "You're absolutely starved."

You rolled his eyes and sank down on the lino, looking as starved as he could. The young man opened the fridge and got out a cold curried egg and a Vegeburger and quite a lot of walnut-and-celery salad. You ate it all up and hiccupped. Then he went to the door and stood with his nose pressed against it.

"Want to go out, do you?" asked the young man, and opened the door. You ran out onto the patio, paused to raise his leg against a bay tree in a tub, then squeezed through the wrought-iron railings into an alley which led to the street.

"Well, that's nice, isn't it," said the young man crossly. "I thought you were going to be *my* dog."

You did not look back. The walnut salad was making him feel a little strange, and

he hiccupped all the way back to Barney's van.

"Hello, you," said Barney, and gave him the last of his bacon butty. And You felt much better.

Chapter 4

The next day, as Barney was trying to buy a car whose engine had fallen out and sell three spare wheels and a battery, You decided that the walnut salad hadn't been so bad after all. But this time, he would be careful about where he lay down. He trotted quite a long way through the shopping centre, and at last came to a pet shop which sold canaries and frozen tripe and chewy things shaped like slippers. It smelt wonderful.

You lay down carefully, and waited. People went into the shop and came out with bird seed and pond weed and the occasional hamster, but none of them took any notice of the brown dog lying on the pavement. Pet-lovers, he thought, were a hard-hearted lot. Then at last he heard the magic words.

"Poor *thing*!" It was a woman's voice, rich and plummy. "Poor *darling*! He's so *thin*!"

You glanced up, but found himself face to face with a fat Pekinese which tried to bite his nose. You growled at it and shut his eyes again. The Pekinese was snatched up by the women. "Pong, that's naughty," she scolded, shaking him. "*Rude*." You, still flat on the pavement, sniggered to himself at the thought of a dog called Pong.

"I'll be back in one moment, darling," the women said to him. "Just as soon as I've put this naughty doggie in the car. Don't you move."

You did not move. The Pekinese had smelt of absolutely delicious food. He heard a car door slam, then the woman came back with a man in dark green trousers who carried a rug. "Carefully, James," she said to the man as he put the rug down and heaved You on to it. "He may be hurt."

You found himself being laid tenderly on the back seat of a huge car which, unlike Barney's van, had no rattles or squeaks, and smelt of leather and perfume instead of oil and grass and old rope. The perfume made him sneeze. The woman sat beside him, restraining the muttering Pekinese. "To the vet, James," she said. "Quickly!"

When the car stopped, You was carried into a brightly lit room which smelled strongly of disinfectant. This was not what he had planned, You thought. He lifted his head and gazed round him suspiciously. "Oh, good," said the woman. "A flicker of life."

A man in a white coat lifted You on to a table then felt him all over and looked in his mouth and in his ears and took his temperature, which You regarded as a great indignity.

"Nothing wrong with him as far as I can see," said the man. "He's in pretty good condition. Got fleas, though." And he took a can of evil-smelling stuff and sprayed it all over You's fur. "And he could have worms," went on the man. "I'll give him a jab for that. Easier than tablets, if a little more expensive."

"Never mind the expense," said the woman. And in the next instant, You found that a needle was being stuck into his rear end. He gave a yelp of protest.

"All done," said the man cheerfully. "Now, don't feed this dog too much, Madam, will you? We don't want problems with obesity and smelly breath like we've had with the Peke."

You gave the man in the white coat a nasty look. This whole thing had been a big mistake, he decided. As soon as he got out of here, he was going straight home to Barney.

But the man in the green uniform wrapped You in the rug and carried him out to the car despite his wriggles, and

locked him in the boot. "Poor sweet," he heard the woman say, "he can't help having fleas, but they could be *such* a nuisance in the Bentley."

Next time the car stopped, You was carried into a very large kitchen where a woman in an apron said, "Oh, my goodness, Madam, what have you got there?"

"A faller by the wayside," said Madam. "A little waif. Perhaps some minced chicken, Gladys, in case his tummy is upset. And I dare say he could manage the rest of the veal fricassée."

You managed the fricassée and the chicken, and some cold salmon as well. Pong watched him as he ate, snarling and snuffling, then gobbled up several prawn crackers and a bowl of milk, eyes bulging with jealousy.

"I shall call him Pilgrim," announced the woman, gazing fondly at You. "Have you ever read a book called *Pilgrim's Progress*, Gladys? No? What a pity. It is all about a brave little chap who struggles through adversity, or so they tell me. Just like our new doggie. Come along, Pilgrim, I'll show you the garden."

You followed her through the back door. It looked like a park rather than a garden, he thought. Flowers bloomed in neat beds and the grass was very short. And all around it, he noticed at once, there was a high wall. He was a prisoner.

"Gladys, watch out in case he Does Anything," the woman commanded.

"Yes, Madam," said Gladys. "Same as Pong. I'll send for James to clear it up."

You almost blushed. He was beginning to feel very worried. This game had gone on for much too long.

Chapter 5

He spent that night slithering about on a
bean bag with a very clean flowered cover.
It rustled every time he moved, and Pong
snored through his flat nose. In the
morning, Gladys sprayed him with
another lot of evil-smelling stuff. "Just
in case," she said, then gave him a large
bowl of porridge with sardines, and a
handful of dog biscuits. Then he was let
out in the garden, and was later scolded
by James for Doing Something under a
prickly bush where it was difficult to
reach.

There were more biscuits at lunchtime,
with chopped-up ham and a bit of
chocolate, and then Madam arrived.

"Nasty day for walkies," she told them.
"Rainy-rainy! We'll need our coats, won't
we!" And she produced something made
of tartan plastic and put it on You,
buckling it under his tummy and across
his chest so that he couldn't scratch it off.
She also put a brass-studded leather
collar round his neck, and attached a
strong lead to it. Then she took both dogs
out to the car.

They drove to a place which You had never seen before, with huge grassy spaces and a lake, and thin-legged animals with horns on their heads. You wanted to chase them, but he felt such a fool in the plastic coat that he could hardly move at all, though Pong pottered about quite happily in his, looking like a woodlouse in a kilt.

The food in Madam's house was good, You had to admit. He had never eaten so much, and it was always delicious. And, as the days went by, he began to get used to the wall which kept him a prisoner in the garden. Every time he was taken for a walk on a sunny day, without the dreadful coat, he would run and run, trying to find a way out, but he always came to a closed gate or a high railing, and James would catch him and clip the lead to his collar, and when Madam was not listening, he called You a blasted obstinate hound.

Chapter 6

Gradually, You began to feel less energetic. As he got fatter, it was difficult to run about so much, and he found himself getting out of breath. He took to sleeping more, and, although the evil-smelling stuff had got rid of his fleas, he sat in the autumn sunshine and scratched at the studded leather collar which made his neck itch.

And then, as he sat scratching one day, a strangely exciting scent came drifting faintly to You's nose. Old rope – grass clippings – oil. He began to bark furiously.

"Good boy," said James approvingly as
he went to the high wrought-iron gate in
the wall. "That's right. You send 'em
packing. No," he said to Barney who
stood outside, "we do not want any knives
sharpened."

"Would you have any trouble with the
car?" asked Barney hopefully. "I can do
you a lovely reconditioned engine. Run
like a dream, it will. Cheap."

"We *never* have trouble with the car," said James haughtily, while You barked and barked, scrabbling at the gate and trying to get through it.

Barney looked at him and said, "Funny – I used to have a dog like that. Young dog he was, though. Healthy. Not a fat old thing like that one. Would you want your lawn mowed?"

"Does the lawn *look* as if it needs to be mowed?" asked James with contempt.

"Not right at the moment," admitted Barney, "but grass is terrible stuff, you know, it keeps on growing. How about telling your fortune? No, I can see you have all you could wish for. Ah, well." He shrugged cheerfully and turned away to the van.

You's barking changed to a frantic whining, and he attacked the gate more desperately. "Want to see him off?" asked James. "Good boy. Go on, then – bite him!" And he opened the gate.

You rushed out, but Barney hopped quickly into the van and slammed the door, then drove off down the road. You tore after him.

"Pilgrim!" shouted James. "Come here! *Pilgrim*! Oh, blast the stupid hound." And he went to get his bike and the dog-lead and a handful of tempting biscuits.

You ran and ran. He was soon gasping for breath. He almost caught up with the van when it stopped at traffic lights, but then it drove away again and he was nearly under the wheels of a bus as he tried to follow it. He retreated to the safety of the pavement and saw the van disappearing into the distance. He sat beside a litter-bin with his fat sides heaving and his tongue hanging out.

"Poor thing!" said a passing schoolboy
kindly – and You at once got up and
staggered on. Those words had got him
into too much trouble already. Glancing
over his shoulder, he saw James
approaching, pedalling fast, and ducked
down an alleyway to avoid him. He kept
going, skulking between people's feet
and behind prams, but at last the shops
began to close and people made their way
home.

You sat down and sniffed the air carefully, but there was no trace of Barney's van any more. And he was lost.

In Madam's house, he thought, it would be feeding time. Pong would be gobbling up a piled plateful of chicken livers or sweet and sour pork with fishy noodles. Pong was keen on that sort of thing. You found his mouth watering at the thought. He nosed at an empty crisps' packet and sniffed hopefully at a couple of dustbins, but they only smelt of ash and beer cans.

Chapter 7

That night, for the first time in months, You slept out in the open, on some dead leaves under a tree in a churchyard. In the morning, he drank some water from a stone vase at the feet of a statue, then started to walk again. He was stiff after yesterday's running, but his breath seemed to come more easily this morning. He broke into a trot. He did not know where he was going, but he felt sure that he was following Barney's van.

By the end of that day, You was seriously hungry. He paused outside a butcher's shop, where the smell of home-cooked ham was so delicious that it made him feel quite faint. The butcher looked at him as he came out to close the shop, and said to a passing policeman, "Reckon that's a stray. I don't like dogs sniffing round my doorway. Unhygienic."

"He looks a bit fat for a stray," said the policeman, but he bent down and clicked his fingers. "Come here, you," he said.

You was so pleased to hear his name spoken that he wagged his tail and approached obediently. The policeman grabbed him by Madam's collar and read the engraved disc, then smiled. "He's a stray all right," he said. "There's a reward out for this one – lady came into the station to report him missing. Posh bird in a chauffeur-driven car."

"Well, I saw him first," said the butcher.

"You just wanted him shifted from your shop," said the policeman, "and that's what I'm doing. Come on, dog."

But You was in a panic. He did not want to be taken anywhere by anyone — and it came to his mind that Barney, for some reason, had never been very keen on policemen. He pulled backwards, jerking his head from side to side, and the collar came up tightly over his ears — and then suddenly he was free. He ran off as fast as he could, and did not stop running until it was dark, and he was too tired to run any further.

Panting, You sat down and stared about him. There were no shops here, and no houses, just tall blocks of flats with empty spaces in between them, and muddy grass. It was starting to rain. There was nowhere to give a tired dog some shelter for the night. You got up and walked on.

At last he came to a tarmac space where a lot of lorries stood parked for the night. They smelt comfortingly of oil, and You crept under one of them and curled up on a flattened cardboard box. He felt terribly empty, but at least he was out of the rain. In another few moments, he was asleep.

Chapter 8

In the morning, he was woken by a powerful blast of pop music, which seemed to come from directly above his head. Then the lorry's engine started with a deafening roar and a cloud of blue smoke. You shot out from underneath the lorry and ran off again.

When he came to a stop, he found that his back felt oddly sticky. He sat down and sniffed at himself, and discovered that he was streaked with black oil from underneath the lorry. He found some earth and rolled in it thoroughly to try and rub the oil off, but it left him looking like a doormat on which several people had wiped muddy boots.

All that day You ran, pausing sometimes to sniff at a likely smelling dustbin or to gaze hopefully at a child with a packet of sweets, but nobody wanted to share anything with a dog so plastered with oil and earth. By the next morning, after a night spent crouched under a barrow on a building-site, You was beginning to wonder if he would ever eat again. He was quite a lot thinner. It was a cold day, and nobody sat in the park with sandwiches. Nobody fed the ducks, either, and they swam far out in the pond, up-ending themselves to guddle for edible things in the water. You watched them enviously. He almost thought of guddling himself, but he wasn't sure if it would work without a beak and feathers.

Then he realised something. He knew this park. He had been here before, many times. He remembered the rubbish bin beside the bandstand, and the seat where a lady had hit him with her handbag for molesting her chihuahua. He sat down with his nose in the air and his eyes shut, trying hard to detect even the faintest whiff of oil and grass and old rope, but the reek of oil from his own coat made it impossible. It would be better, he thought, if he smelled of something quite different. But what?

He set off again, more carefully this time, his nose twitching as he searched for something to roll in, and for something to eat – and, of course, for Barney's van.

He left the town behind him and trotted along a road which had a grass verge instead of a pavement. Looking through the hedge, he could see a field on the other side, and after a while, he came to a farm gate.

You paused and sniffed. From the farmyard, there came a wonderful smell of dung. He wriggled under the gate, avoided a fierce cockerel, and made his way to the dungheap, where he rolled and rubbed and scrubbed until the smell of oil on his coat had completely disappeared. He smelt very strongly of dung instead, but that, he thought, would not confuse him when he was trying to find the oily scent of Barney's van.

He stood up and shook himself – and at that moment, the farmer came round the corner of the barn, with a gun over his arm and two black-and-white collies at his heels.

"Gerroff!" shouted the farmer – and the two collies rushed forward with bared teeth. You fled, cramming himself under the gate and rushing out into the road. *Eeeeek!* There was a scream of brakes –

and You, leaping out of the way of a van which had so nearly hit him, was overwhelmed by the beautiful perfume of oil, grass-clippings and old rope.

Barney leaned out of the window and said, "Now, there is an idjit dog. Nearly got itself squashed flat."

Chapter 9

You rushed at him, whining frantically.

"Wait a minute," said Barney thoughtfully.
"Didn't I see an advert for a dog like
that?" He fished out a piece of newspaper
which was wrapping up a bundle of
second-hand hacksaw blades and
scanned it. "Ah, yes, here we are. 'For the
safe return of Pilgrim, brown dog with
large feet, five pounds.' Now, there's a lot
I could do with five pounds." He looked
at You again. "Could be the one," he said.
"A bit like the one I used to have, only
mine wasn't so smelly. And he was
thinner." He got out of the van with a
piece of old rope. "Come here, Pilgrim or
whatever your name is," he said.

You felt puzzled as Barney tied the rope
round his neck and led him to the back
of the van. Surely, in just these few
months, he hadn't forgotten what You
was called? But human beings were a bit
odd sometimes. You jumped in and lay
down beside the knife-sharpening
machine. Barney would probably
remember, given time.

"Oy!" shouted the farmer from the gate,
where the collies still snarled. "If that's
your dog, just look after it in future. Look
at the mess it's made of my dungheap!

Muck all over the place."

"Sorry about that," said Barney. He started the van's engine, then added, "You couldn't do with some nice hacksaw blades, could you?"

"No, I could not," said the farmer, and shifted his gun to hold it in both hands. Barney drove away.

You lay contentedly in the back. Soon, he thought, they would stop and make a camp fire somewhere, and perhaps Barney would give him something to eat.

They drove for quite a long time. But when the van stopped and Barney opened its rear door, You looked out then shrank back in dismay at the sight of the ornamental wrought-iron gate and the clipped lawn.

"Come on," said Barney, yanking at You's rope. "Ah, there y'are, sir, I've brought the dog." James had come to the gate and was frowning distastefully. "Wait here," he ordered. "I will ask Madam."

You did his best to climb back into the van, but Barney held the rope firmly. "I've found your dog for you, Missus," You heard him say. "Come for the reward. Five pounds, it says here in the paper."

"Oh, no," said Madam. "My Pilgrim was a nice, clean dog. And quite plump." She and Pong both wrinkled their noses as they looked at the dung-plastered You.

"Ah, but you can't call this dog thin, Missus," argued Barney, peering at You short-sightedly. "He's your dog all right. Seen him here before, I did, just a few days ago."

"Nonsense," said Madam. "That dog doesn't even know me. Look at it, trying to get back into your van. And it smells absolutely disgusting. You should be ashamed of yourself, trying to get five pounds for some filthy cur like that. I've a good mind to telephone the authorities."

"Don't do that, Missus," said Barney. "No call for that." He bundled You back into the van. "Nothing wrong with a bit of muck," he added as he got into the driving seat. "Would you like some for your garden? I know where there's a good pile of it."

"*Go away!*" said Madam and James together. Barney shrugged and drove off.

Chapter 10

It was evening when he stopped again, in a grassy place by a river. He let You out of the van, took off the piece of rope, and pointed at the river. "In," he said.

Helped by a shove from Barney with a yard-broom, You waded into the water and floundered about until all the dung was washed off his coat, and all the earth and most of the oil. Barney scrubbed the last of it off with the yard-broom and some engine-cleaning stuff and sent You back into the river again, then rubbed him dry with an old sack. After that, he lit a fire and boiled up the black kettle and cooked a panful of sausages. You watched, dribbling, while Barney ate.

At last, Barney fished a cooling sausage out of the pan. "Here, you," he said, "catch!"

You was so delighted to hear the sound of his name at last that he missed the sausage, hungry though he was, while he leapt up at Barney to give him a big, wet kiss.

"Great idjit," said Barney as You retrieved the sausage and gulped it down. "My old one would never have missed a bit of food. You and him are like as two peas, though." He threw the dog another sausage. "If you were just a bit thinner, I'd think you were him."

You looked up, wagging his tail at this repeated use of his name, and Barney shook his head regretfully. "Pity I never gave him a name," he said. "Then I could call you by it and see if you knew it."

You was not sure what Barney was talking about, but he was so happy to be recognised at last that he rested his chin on Barney's knee and gazed up at him adoringly.

"Can't be," said Barney with regret. "The old one never did that. Still, you're a nice dog. You'll do."

You curled up at his feet, and Barney sat and gazed into the fire until it burned low and the autumn night turned chilly. Then he got up. "Time to turn in," he said. "Come on, you."

Snug and warm beside Barney on an old sack in the van, You yawned happily. He would never go off with anyone else, as long as he lived.